the **BAD GUYS**

in

· AARON BLABEY ·

the **BAD GUYS**

in

SCHOLASTIC INC.

OPEN WIDE
AND
SAY ARRRGH!

Pssst!
Hey, Wolfie . . .

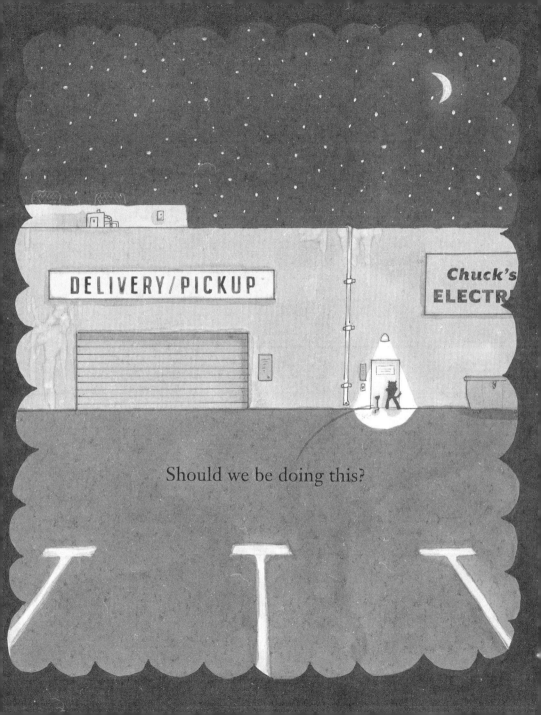

Should we be doing this?

I have my momennnnnnngghh . . .
MOMENNNNNGGHH . . .
MOMENNNNGGHHHH
I'M SORRY... WHAT DID YOU SAY?

• CHAPTER 1 •

THE DENTAL APPOINTMENT

LETMEGO! GETOFFME!
ISN'T THIS A BLAST?!
MMMMM!

Look, I'm just gonna say it . . . your conversation skills kind of **STINK**, you know?
MMM MMMM!

No, no. STOP. You're just embarrassing yourself. I'll take it from here.

Am I saying that right now?
The One?

GREAT!

Well, young lady,

DELUSIONAL
AMBITIONS

are all well and good,
but they won't help you much
if you don't take care of your . . .

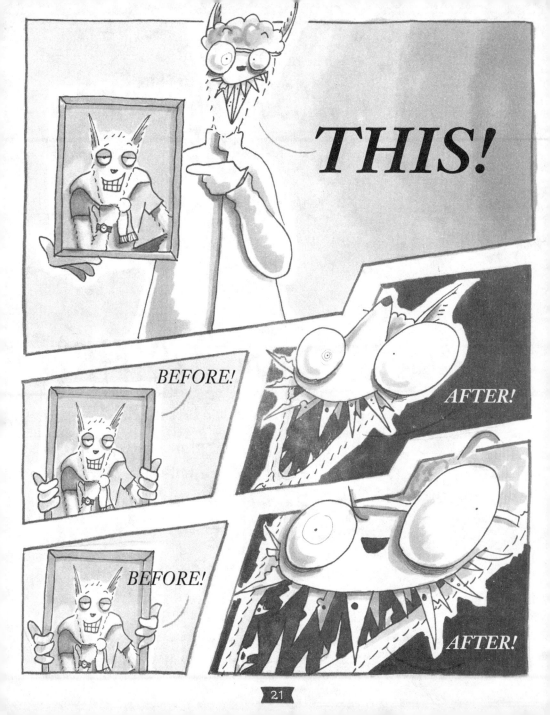

I, TOO, was once a

HIDEOUS ABOMINATION.

But my **MASTER** gave me

powers beyond my wildest dreams

and I became the

NEXT-LEVEL ORAL HYGIENIST

you see before you today!

And for a LIMITED TIME ONLY,
I'm offering a

FULL DENTAL MAKEOVER

for the LOW, LOW PRICE of . . .

JUST HEARING YOU SCREAM.

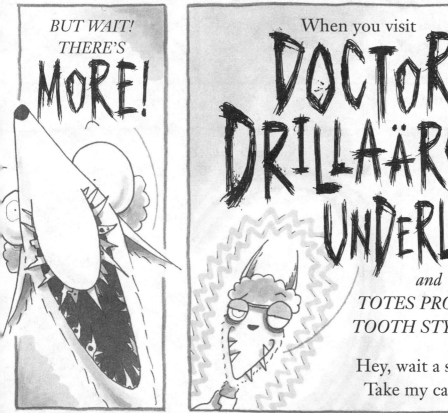

BUT WAIT! THERE'S MORE!

When you visit

DOCTOR DRILLAÄRGH, UNDERLORD

and
TOTES PROFESH
TOOTH STYLIST—

Hey, wait a second.
Take my card . . .

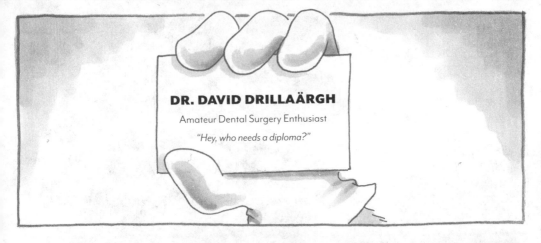

Well, GO ON!
It's not going to
refuel itself.

And no stopping for snacks!

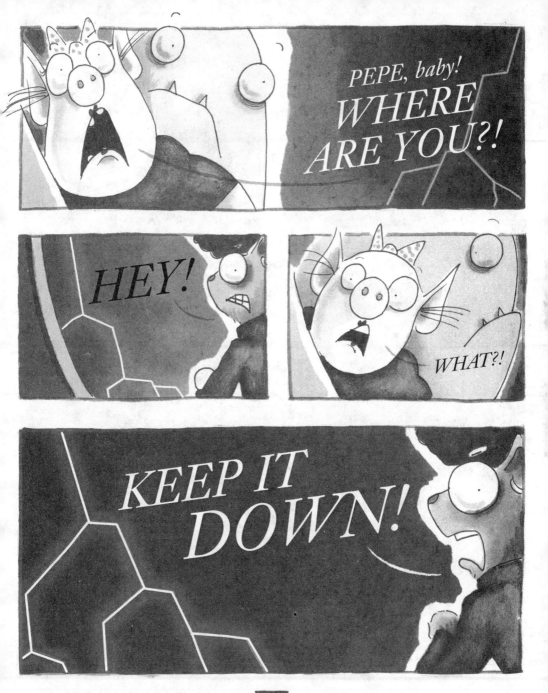

The only thing we have
going for us is the
**ELEMENT OF
SURPRISE.**

If **SNAKE** sees us coming,
we're done for.
And **FOX** isn't here
to help us this time.

If he gets us, we're *his*.

He's surprisingly robust.
He'll be fine.

You two go back a long way, huh?

How'd you meet?

We were just kids, really . . .

I was eating out one night . . .

. . . when this little guy came out of nowhere
and started screaming that I'd stolen his meal.

SMACK!

I informed him that he was mistaken.

He considered this for a moment
. . . and then said,

"Sure, *chico*. You have
that little entrée.
You've put me in the
mood for . . ."

A MAIN COURSE.

What a beautiful story.

HEY, LOOK!
IS THAT . . . ?

IT'S HIM!

OK.
This is our one chance.
Let's grab him fast.

And don't forget, this is
all about the element of . . .

· CHAPTER 3 ·
THE UTENSIL WITHIN

Breathe, Fluffit.

How often do you get to watch a

VELOCIRAPTOR

have a conversation with a

CHAIN SAW MANIAC?
IN SPACE?!

This is compelling stuff.

MILT!

SHOW ME...

Um . . .

Dang . . .

Is that . . . ?

Dang . . .

That looks like . . .

FOOF!

Dang . . .

Wait . . . what?!
He's just . . . a
BABY SPOON?!

Called "Dickie"?

Dang . . .

He's not as scary as he seems!
He's not some unbeatable MONSTER.
He just **LOOKED** like one.

It's like SNAKE.
Underneath, *on the inside*,
he's just plain old Snake.

We can BEAT these guys!

All we have to do is
**NOT BE
AFRAID**
of them.

Hold up.

If any of **US** tried what the dinosaur
just did, we'd be *dead*.

We wouldn't have even made it outside the ship.

And even if we *did* survive being

CRUSHED BY SPACE,

we'd have been

CHOPPED
TO PIECES.

What just happened didn't
make any sense.

We should
TOTALLY
be afraid of them.

· CHAPTER 4 ·
DARK AND WEIRD

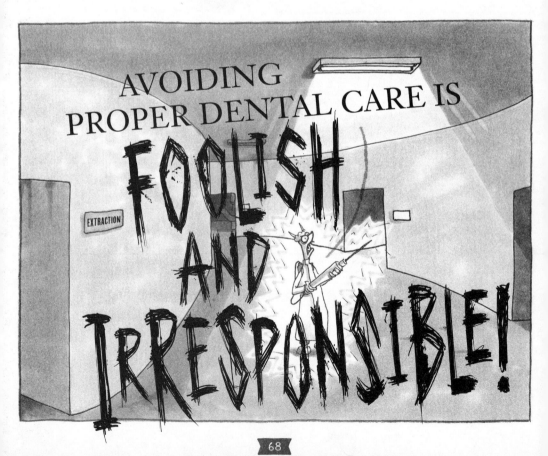

AVOIDING PROPER DENTAL CARE IS

EXTRACTION

FOOLISH AND IRRESPONSIBLE!

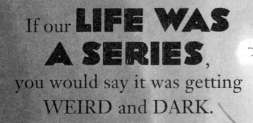

If our **LIFE WAS A SERIES**, you would say it was getting WEIRD and DARK.

Like, a lot weirder and darker than those highly accessible early books . . .

It's because we're getting close to . . . *you know who.*

The **HEAVY METAL CENTIPEDE?**

Trouble is, other than Piranha, no one knows where the next **DOORWAY** is . . .

I do . . .

I'm a **BAT**.

And sorry—full disclosure—I was

EAVESDROPPING.

I heard everything you said.

Did you say you
know where

**THE
DOORWAY**

is?

Will you take us to the DOORWAY?

Yes, of course.

But it IS a bit **INCONVENIENT** because I'm supposed to be doing **SOMETHING ELSE**.

I'm not trying to make you feel guilty. I just can't hide my feelings and I feel compelled to share them.

Can't help it.

WHAT?!

You seem like the **SLIGHTLY LESS INTELLIGENT MEMBER** of the group.

I deeply regret having said that out loud, but I just . . .

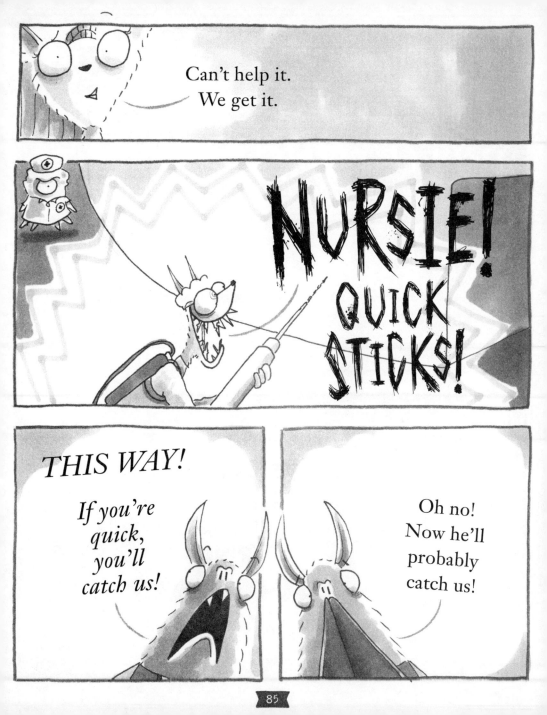

WHAT IS WRONG WITH YOU?!

I'm pathologically honest and . . .

WHAT were you supposed to be doing? Instead of taking us to **THE DOORWAY?**

I'm supposed to wait until

THE ONE

arrives.

· CHAPTER 5 ·
WHO NEEDS MAGIC HANDS?

Oh no . . .

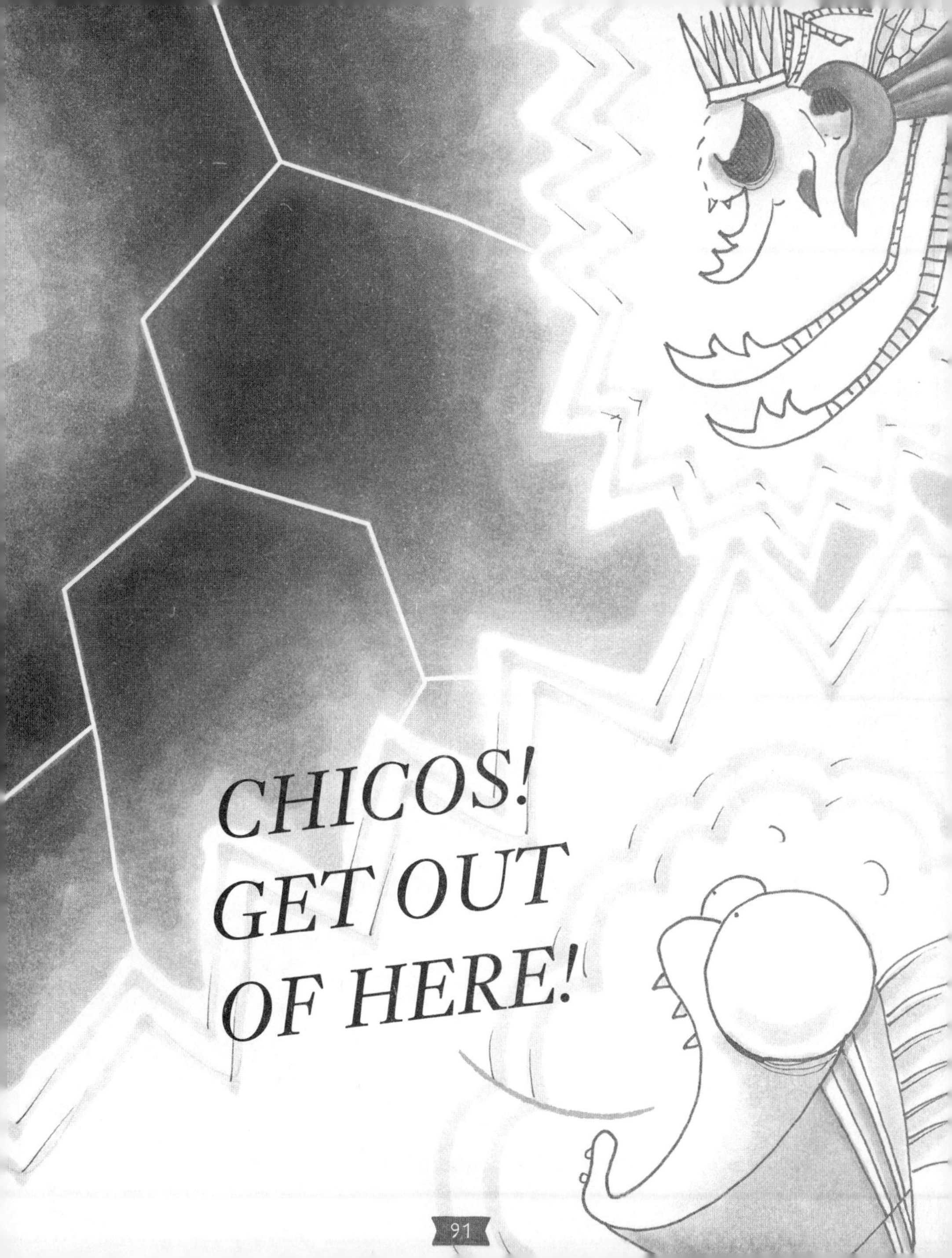
CHICOS! GET OUT OF HERE!

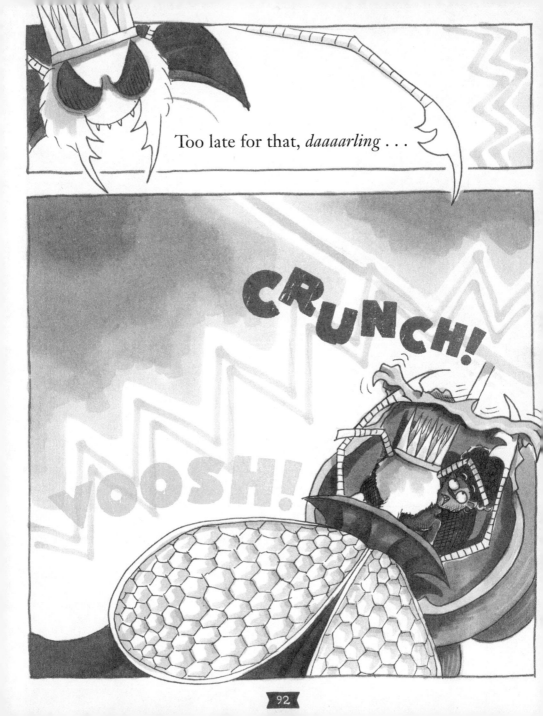

You guys are SO predictable, you know that?

GET OUT HERE AND JOIN THE PARTY.

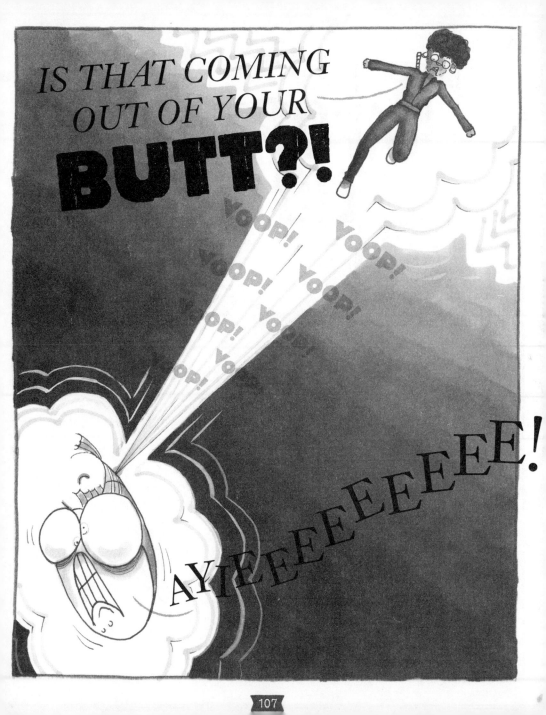

· CHAPTER 6 ·
IMPORTANT HOW?

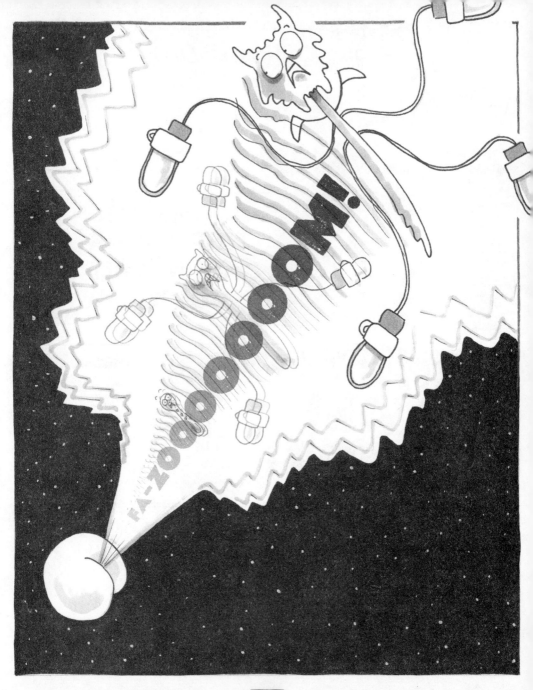

And there goes **DICKIE**, the **INTERGALACTIC BABY SPOON.**

If anyone needed proof this is a less important subplot, *there it goes . . .*

WRONG!

· CHAPTER 7 ·
THE TRUTH TELLER

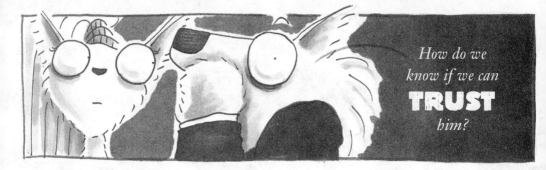

Just letting you know that as a **BAT**, I rely on my really **QUITE EXCELLENT HEARING** and, accordingly, I can once again hear **EVERYTHING** that you're saying.

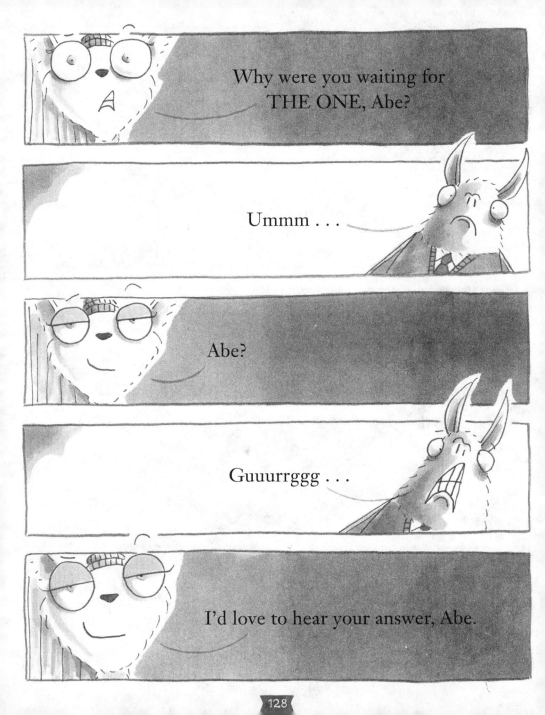

Iyyyyyyiiiieeeee . . .

. . . WAS WAITING FOR **THE ONE** BECAUSE **I** AM ONE OF **THE OTHERS** AND **THE ONE** CAN'T SUCCEED WITHOUT **THE OTHERS** SO THAT'S WHY I WAS WAITING BUT I **SHOULDN'T** HAVE SAID THAT BECAUSE I'M ONE OF **THE OTHERS**.

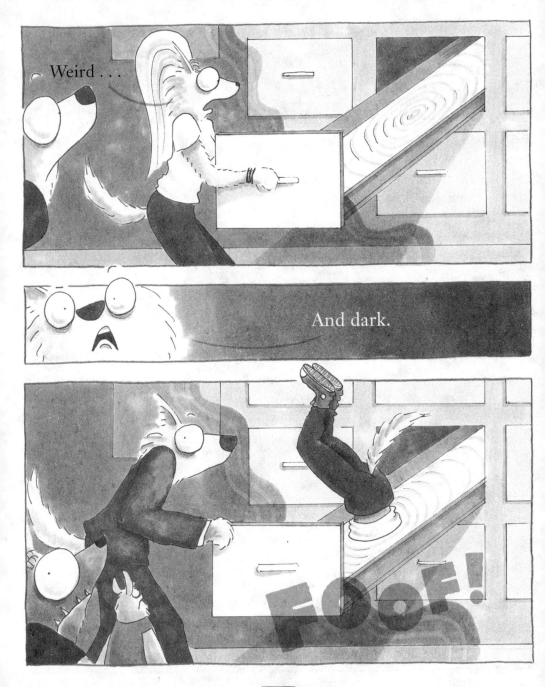

Well, nice to meet you. Good luck with everything.

· CHAPTER 8 ·
ONE AT A TIME, PLEASE

PIRANHA! WIDEN THE BEAM! YOU NEED TO HIT ALL THREE OF US!

IMPOSSIBLE!

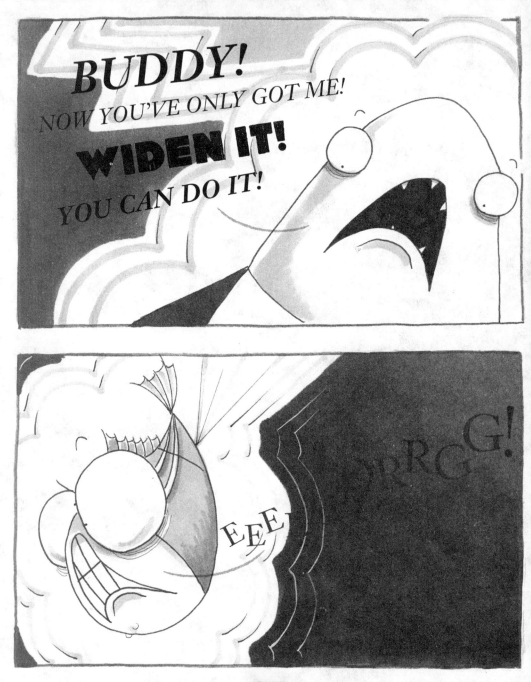

DON'T YOU DO IT, PIRANHA!
KITTY, BABY, THIS MAKES SENSE . . .
IT DOES!
NO!
WE'LL BE OK. SOMEHOW . . . SOMEDAY . . .
IT'LL ALL BE OK IN THE END . . .

I forgot how rad these helicopters are. This is *fun*.

SMACK!

GRRRAAARRGHH!

· CHAPTER 9 ·
THE OTHERS

This is the place?

Where are they?

Buck?!

Oh, quit yo' fussin' . . .

And you're going to take us to *The Others*?

Not sure I follow . . .

WHERE ARE ALL "THE OTHERS"?

· CHAPTER 10 ·
ABE IN THE WOODS

Oh, she's **BAD**.
And when she's around,
everything turns bad.

Wonderful.

Do you know where the
next Doorway is?

EEEEEEEEE!

Everyone, stay completely silen—

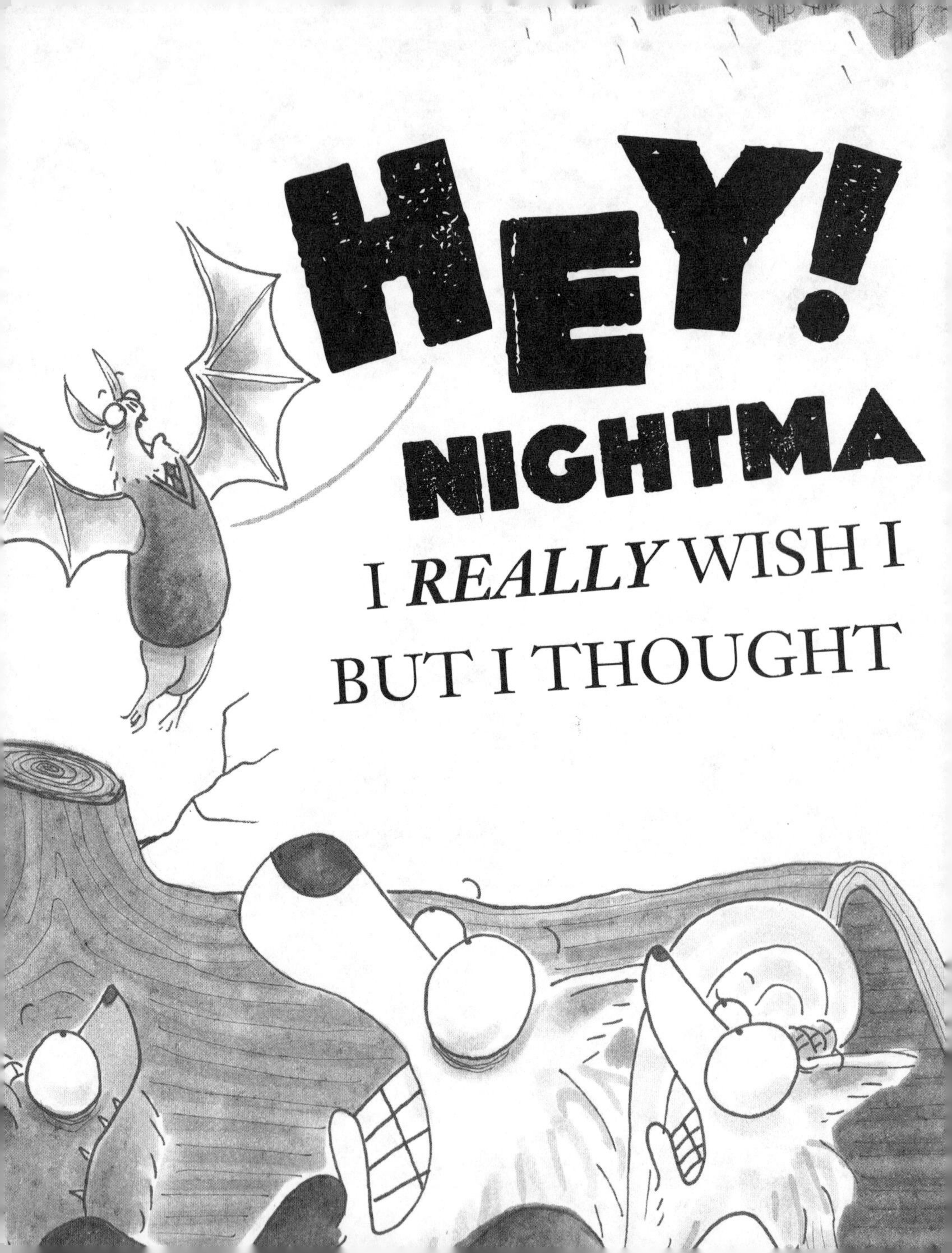
HEY!
NIGHTMA
I *REALLY* WISH I
BUT I THOUGHT

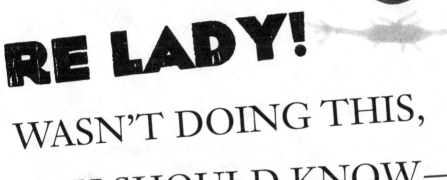

RE LADY!

WASN'T DOING THIS,

YOU SHOULD KNOW—

WE'RE
RIGHT OVER
HERE!

TO BE CONTINUED . . .

OK, so just to **WRAP IT ALL UP . . .**

• There's something completely **EVIL** in the woods.

• Shark and Hogwild are **DOOMED.**

• The Chain Saw Guy is a **SPOON.**

• And **BUCK THUNDERS** is our only hope.

We hope you've enjoyed this series.
Good luck with all your future endeavors.

Just kidding.